n Level 0, **Step 2** builds c
n Step 1 and focuses on t.

a   t   p

pecial features:

honically decodable text
uilds reading confidence

nort
ntences
ith simple
nguage

epetition
sounds in
fferent words

Pippa tips the pip in the tin.

I tip it in.

Story Words

Can you match these words to the pictures?

tin
Pippa
pip
pats
sit

Tricky Words

These tricky words are in the story you have just read. They cannot be sounded out. Can you memorize them and read them super fast?

the
I
no

Summary page to
reinforce learning

Practice of words that
cannot be sounded out

Educational Consultant: Geraldine Taylor
Phonics and Book Banding Consultant: Kate Ruttle

LADYBIRD BOOKS

UK | USA | Canada | Ireland | Australia
India | New Zealand | South Africa

Ladybird Books is part of the Penguin Random House group of companies
whose addresses can be found at global.penguinrandomhouse.com.

www.penguin.co.uk www.puffin.co.uk www.ladybird.co.uk

First edition published 2020
001

Printed in China

A CIP catalogue record for this book is available from the British Library

ISBN: 978-0-241-40505-5

All correspondence to
Ladybird Books
Penguin Random House Children's
80 Strand, London WC2R 0RL

Pippa and
the Pip

Written by Catherine Baker
Illustrated by Ela Smietanka

It is a pip, Pippa!

A pip and a tin.

9

Pippa pats it.

Pat! Pat! Tap! Tap!

10

11

Pippa sits and sits.

No pip!

12

13

It is Pippa's pip!

14

15

Story Words

Can you match these words
to the pictures?

tin

Pippa

pip

pats

sit

Tricky Words

These tricky words are in the story you have just read. They cannot be sounded out. Can you memorize them and read them super fast?

the

I

no

Pippa and Pippin

Written by Catherine Baker
Illustrated by Ela Smietanka

20

21

Nan sits Pippa on Pippin.

23

Pippa sits, and Nan sits.

Nan naps.

A nit nips Pippin.
Pippa tips!

27

Pippa and Pippin tip.

Pippa and Nan sit and sip!

Sip! Sip!

Story Words

Can you match these words to the pictures?

nit

Nan

Pippin

Pippa

sip

Stories and rhymes in this book

IS IT A BIRD...?

THE DIVING CONTEST

THE DARING DUCKS' DIVING SONG

THE PERFECT POND

DUCK LUCK

THE TREASURE HUNT

YOUNG AT HEART

MUM TO THE RESCUE

SWEET DREAMS, DARING DUCKS!

· Published by Ladybird Books Ltd
27 Wrights Lane London W8 5TZ
A Penguin Company
© LADYBIRD BOOKS LTD MCMXCIX
Produced for Ladybird Books Ltd by Nicola Baxter and Amanda Hawkes
The moral rights of the author/illustrator have been asserted
LADYBIRD and the device of a Ladybird are trademarks of Ladybird Books Ltd

The Daring Ducks

by Nicola Baxter

illustrated by Terry Norridge

IS IT A BIRD...?

What's that
whizzing
through
the sky?

Great Grandma Daring
Duck's flying high.

Who's that
working late
at night?
Grandad Daring Duck's
planning his next flight.

Whose parachuting gets nought out of ten?

It's Dad Daring Duck in trouble... again!

Who's that making a daring climb? It's Mum to the rescue one more time.

THE DIVING CONTEST

"Today," said Dad Daring Duck one morning, "I'm going to organize a Daring Diving Contest."

"Wonderful!" said Great Grandma Daring Duck.

"It'll need careful planning," said Grandad Daring Duck.

"Hooray!" "Hooray!" "Hooray!" said the three Daring Ducklings.

And Mum Daring Duck said, "Oh, no, not again," very, very quietly.

After breakfast, Dad wrote out The Rules.

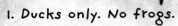

1. Ducks only. No frogs.
2. Each contestant has one dive.
3. The judge's decision is final.
4. The contest organizer is the judge.

The first to
dive was
Great
Grandma
Daring
Duck...

Next came
Grandad
Daring
Duck...

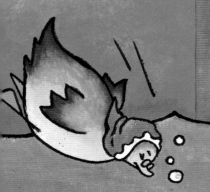

with no
splash at all!

he did
a textbook
dive (with
a textbook).

But Daring
Dad was
keen to win.
He gave
them...

a somersault
with spin,

a double
back-flip,

a loopy loop,

and a triple-twisting
twizzle with tail-wiggle.

If only
the pond had
been bigger...

DOINGGG!

For medical reasons, the judge had to write down his decision:

EVERYONE'S A WINNER! HOORAY!

THE DARING DUCKS' DIVING SONG

One, two, three, four, five,

The Daring Ducks get ready to dive.

Five, four, three, two, one,
Nothing else is so much fun!

THE PERFECT POND

"In olden times," said Grandad Daring Duck one evening, "ducks lived at a place called Perfect Pond."

"What was it like?" asked the Daring Ducklings.

"It had LOTS of fat fish...

and FORESTS of delicious duckweed...

and the frogs were quiet and not fidgety," said Grandad Daring Duck.

"Let's go and find it!" cried the Daring Ducklings, jumping up and down.

"Expeditions need proper planning," warned Grandad.

But the
Daring
Ducklings...

and Dad,
carrying his
binoculars...

and Great
Grandma...

and Mum
carrying
a picnic
basket...

set off
straight
away. So
Grandad
Daring Duck
went too —
with his bag
of emergency
supplies.

They
followed
a footpath
between
the fields...

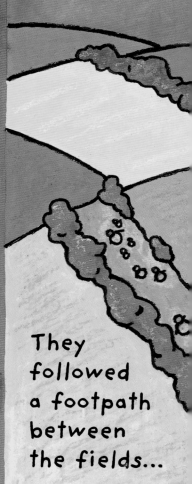

and through the forest...

and over the hills...

until the sun began to set.

And she led
them over
the hills...

and through
the forest...

and across the fields,
until at dawn they came to...

their old familiar pond.
And it was...

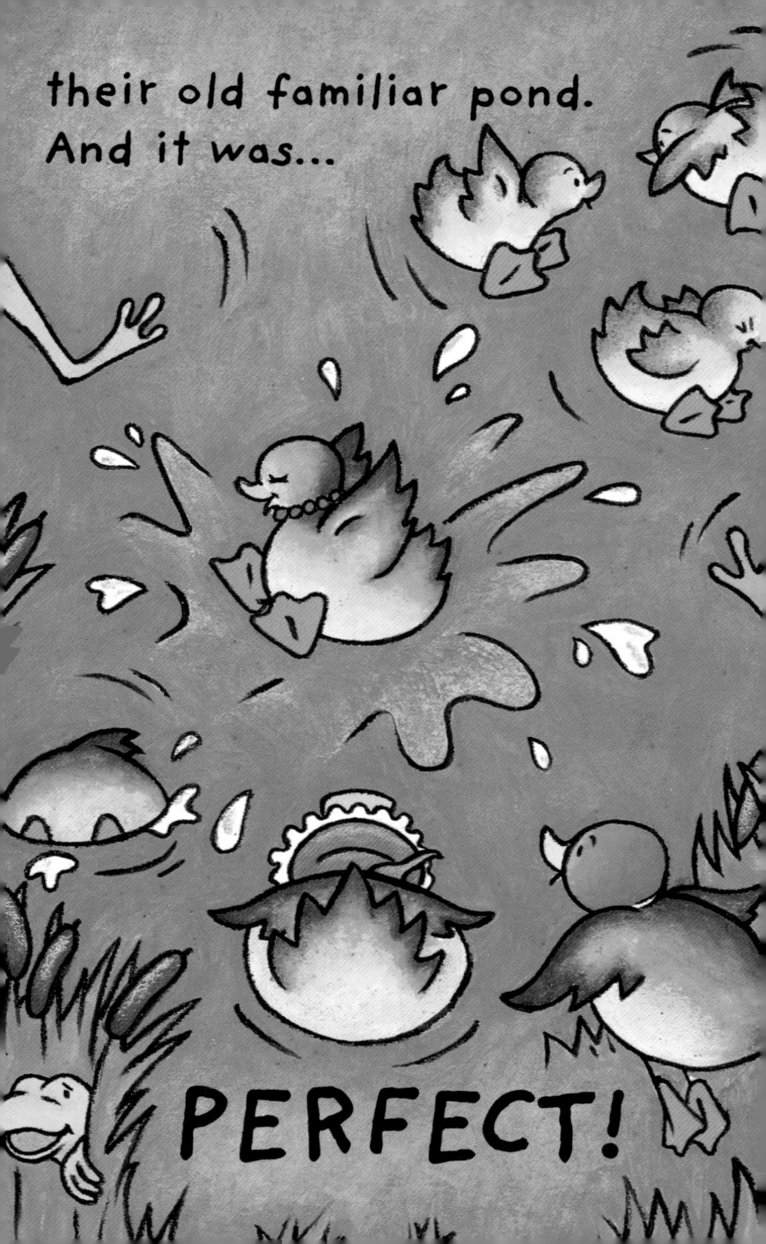

PERFECT!

DUCK LUCK

A Daring Duck
Needs lots of luck.

A cat has *NINE* lives
For safety, you see,

But Daring Ducks
Need SEVENTY-THREE!

THE TREASURE HUNT

"Have you ever dived right to the bottom of the pond, Grandad?" asked the Daring Ducklings one day.

"That would be dangerous," replied Grandad. "Who knows what's down there?"

So the Daring Ducklings asked Mum instead.

"That would be VERY silly," she said. "You three stay where I can see you."

But when the ducklings asked Great Grandma, she said, "WHAT A GOOD IDEA! Follow ME!"

She dived down...

and down...

until she came to the bottom.

"Glubblelub blubbelook!" said Great Grandma, making lots of bubbles.

"Glip!" "Glop!" "Gloop!" said the Daring Ducklings.

Soon the Daring Ducks were gasping and gulping on the surface of the pond.

"What a relief!" cried Daring Mum. But she was curious. "What IS down there?" she asked.

"Exactly the same as up here," said the leading adventurer.

"There are weeds...

and fish...

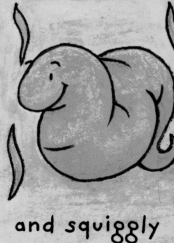

and squiggly things...

YOUNG AT HEART

Great Grandma simply
won't be told
She can't be
daring now
she's old.

She says,
"My wings
WERE once
more whizzy,

But I
believe in
being busy.

I can't stand
here and
talk to you...

I've lots of daring deeds
to do!"

MUM TO THE RESCUE

The Daring Ducks are very careful about cats.

They even prefer frogs to pets that purr.

One day,
the Daring
Ducks heard
a mewing
sound...

but they
couldn't see
a cat until...

they looked
upwards.

"Not me," said Great Grandma Daring Duck.

"Not me," said Daring Dad with a shiver.

"Not me!"
"Not me!"
"Not me!"
said the Daring Ducklings.

"If you want a job doing," muttered Mum, and she got out her climbing gear.

Then up she went.

The Daring
Ducks held
their breath
as Mum
reached the
cat...

who at once
climbed
down all by
himself.

SWEET DREAMS, DARING DUCKS!

At the end
of every
daring day,
The Daring
Ducks all
hug and say,

"Sleep well and dream of
daring deeds...